SEP 1 7 2015

See You Next Year

With love to Esther, Bella, and Charlie. Long may we holiday. — A.L.

For Emily and Henry — T.S.

Text © 2015 Andrew Larsen
Illustrations © 2015 Todd Stewart

Owlkids Books acknowledges the financial support of the Canada Council for the Arts, the Ontario Arts Council, the Government of Canada through the Canada Book Fund (CBF) and the Government of Ontario through the Ontario Media Development Corporation's Book Initiative for our publishing activities.

Published in Canada by
Owlkids Books Inc.
10 Lower Spadina Avenue
Toronto, ON M5V 2Z2

Published in the United States by
Owlkids Books Inc.
1700 Fourth Street
Berkeley, CA 94710

Library and Archives Canada Cataloguing in Publication

Larsen, Andrew, 1960-, author
    See you next year / written by Andrew Larsen ; illustrated by Todd Stewart.

ISBN 978-1-926973-99-9 (bound)

I. Stewart, Todd, 1972-, illustrator  II. Title.

PS8623.A77S43 2015      jC813'.6      C2014-904545-X

Library of Congress Control Number: 2014945471

Edited by: Karen Boersma
Designed by: Karen Powers

Manufactured in Shenzhen, Guangdong, China, in August 2014, by WKT Co. Ltd.
Job #14B0427

A      B      C      D      E      F

Publisher of Chirp, chickaDEE and OWL
www.owlkidsbooks.com

# See You Next Year

Written by ANDREW LARSEN     Illustrated by TODD STEWART

Owlkids Books

EVERY YEAR we take the same roads.

We pass through the same towns.

We arrive at the same beach.

Every year we stay at the same place.

I call it our cottage.

But it's not really a cottage.

It's a motel.

We always come on a Saturday.

We always stay for a week.

We've been coming to the same

place every summer since I was little.

Nothing changes.

That's why I like it.

On Sunday morning I wake up early

so I can watch the tractor on the beach.

The tractor goes round and round, pulling

a beach raker, leaving a swirly design.

Then, the seagulls come.

They walk on the freshly raked sand.

Sometimes they mess it all up.

They hang around until the people arrive, with

their coolers and their towels and all their beach stuff.

Then they go.

It's not long before the beach is a sea of umbrellas.

You can hardly see the swirls or the sand.

This year I made a new friend.

He taught me how to swim.

Well, sort of...

He showed me how to hold my nose
and dive under the waves.

The water isn't deep at the beach.

I can touch the bottom.

But I still wear my life jacket.

Late in the afternoon everyone packs up

their beach stuff and their towels and their coolers.

They take down their umbrellas.

Everyone moves slowly.

They leave the beach as the gulls return.

It's the same every day.

On Monday night we all go to the bandstand in town.

A marching band plays onstage while we sit on
the grass and listen.

Some kids march.

Some dance.

Some of the old people fall asleep.

A bulldog barks when the lady in the marching band
crashes the cymbals.

The old people wake up with a jump.

CRASH!

Woof!

CRASH! CRASH! CRASH!

Woof! Woof! Woof!

On Tuesday it's foggy.

I can't see the water, but I can hear the waves.

I can't see the tractor.

I can't see the gulls.

No one comes to the beach with their umbrellas or their coolers or their towels.

I go to my friend's room to see what he's doing.

He's writing postcards.

He asks if I want to write one, too.

He offers me a postcard and a pen.

The postcard has a picture of the beach.

My friend tells me I can send it to anyone.

Anyone.

On Wednesday our vacation is half-over.

I'm half-happy and half-sad.

On Thursday my new friend and I have nothing to do.

So we dig a hole.

We want to dig all the way to the center of the earth.

We don't quite get there.

But we hit water.

Then it's time for lunch.

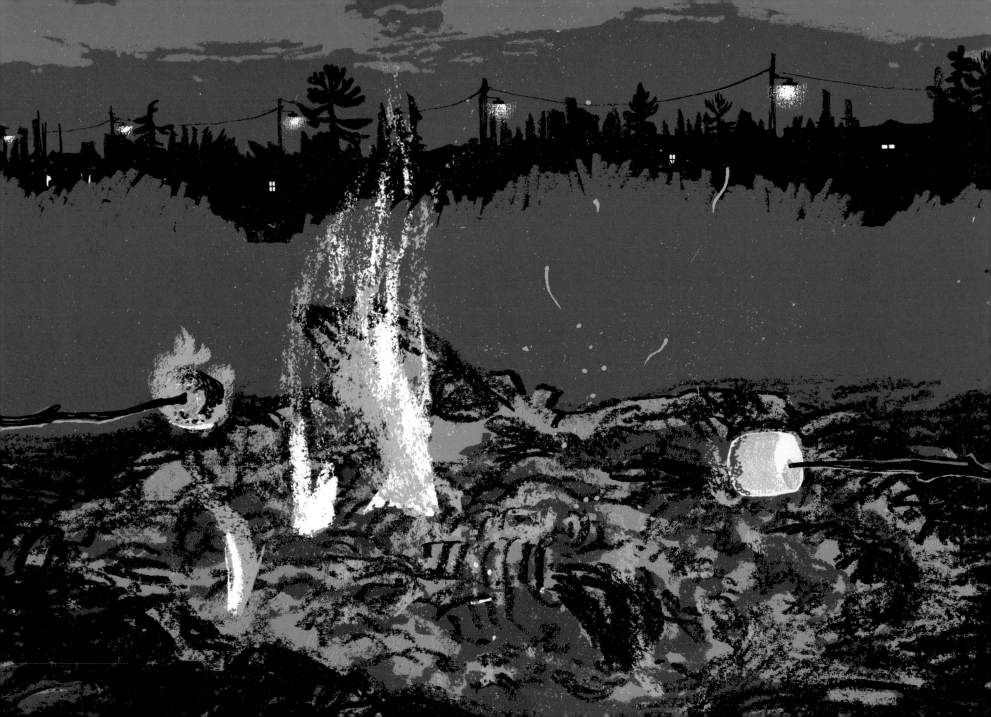

On Friday my holiday is almost over.

I get to stay up late.

So does my friend.

Our parents make a bonfire on the beach.

I find the perfect stick for roasting marshmallows.

I like mine roasted golden brown.

My friend likes his burnt.

I'm going to bring my marshmallow stick home
so I can keep it for next year.

The sky is full of stars.

I see a shooting star.

My friend says it's a satellite.

So I make a satellite wish.

On Saturday morning we pack the car.

It's time to say good-bye.

"See you next year," says my friend.

He's lucky.

He gets to stay for an extra day.

"See you next year," I say back to him.

And then we take the same roads through the same towns until we're back home.

It's good to be home.

It almost seems like we never left.

On Monday something comes in the mail.

It's for me.